DO YOU ENJOY BEING FRIGHTENED?

WOULD YOU RATHER HAVE
NIGHTMARES
INSTEAD OF SWEET DREAMS?

ARE YOU HAPPY ONLY WHEN
SHAKING WITH FEAR?

CONGRATULATIONS ! ! ! !

YOU'VE MADE A WISE CHOICE.

THIS BOOK IS THE DOORWAY
TO ALL THAT MAY FRIGHTEN YOU.

GET READY FOR

COLD, CLAMMY SHIVERS
RUNNING UP AND DOWN YOUR SPINE!

NOW, OPEN THE DOOR–
IF YOU DARE !!!!

Shivers

THE CURSE OF THE NEW KID

M. D. Spenser

Paradise Press, Inc.

Plantation, Florida

ISBN 1-57657-054-1

EXCLUSIVE DISTRIBUTION BY PARADISE PRESS, INC.

Cover Design by George Paturzo
Cover Illustration by Eddie Roseboom

Printed in the U.S.A.

30631

To J.,G., and the twins

THE CURSE OF THE

OF THE

NEW KID

Chapter One

I am cursed.

No matter where I go, no matter what I do, I always get picked on.

I don't get it.

Maybe I have a birthmark on the back of my head that says, "Beat Me Up."

It's been like this all my life. I got beat up in first grade. I got beat up in second grade. We moved when I was in third grade.

I'm 12 years old and this is my eighth school. We move a lot.

My dad is some kind of company big shot. They're always sending him somewhere to straighten things out. He says he's a trouble shooter.

He fixes everybody else's problems, but he can't help me.

"Here's what you do," he tells me. "First day

of school, you make friends with the biggest guy in class. That will keep kids from picking on you, Luke."

That never works. The biggest kid in the school is always the first one to beat me up.

At this school, his name is Huff.

Huff is always wiping his nose with the sleeve of his shirt. He's got little black eyes and lots of zits on his face. Huff is big, and he's just as wide as he is tall.

He calls himself Rough and Tough Huff. And he is.

I could tell the first time he saw me that he hated my guts.

I was walking down the hall at school, trying to find Miss Swimmer's classroom, when I saw him coming toward me.

He's an easy guy to see, because all the other kids get out of the way when they see him coming.

I saw a movie once where an old guy with a beard made the water of a lake move apart so people could walk across the lake without getting wet.

That's what it's like when Huff walks through the school. And then trailing behind him is his gang.

It's not like a real gang. They don't wear all the same color of stuff and they don't have to beat anybody up to join or anything.

They just beat you up for fun.

When I saw them coming toward me, Huff in front and the rest trailing behind him, I knew I was in trouble.

I turned to a locker and started fiddling with the lock like it was my locker and I was trying to figure out the combination.

But it didn't work.

I could smell Huff's breath on me before I heard him say anything. He smells like onions, even in the morning.

"Hey, you. New kid," Huff said.

I gulped, and looked up.

The biggest zit on his face is at the tip of his nose. It was like another eye staring at me. I tried not to stare back.

"What are you looking at, punk?" Huff snarled at me.

"Nothing," I said. "I'm not looking at nothing."

3

Huff snorted and some snot sprayed from his nose.

"Nothing?" he laughed.

It was a mean laugh, not a happy laugh. He turned his head to the bunch of guys behind him who were laughing mean laughs too.

"Nothing, he says. You heard him, didn't you guys? He says I'm nothing."

"Oh no, that's not what I mean," I said quickly.

I could feel it happening all over again.

I felt that familiar hollow feeling in the middle of my guts. The kind of sick feeling just before you throw up, or somebody socks you in the stomach.

"Well, little wussie, that's what you said. You're looking right at me and you say right to my face that you're not looking at nothing. That sounds to me like you're dissing me. Doesn't it sound like he's dissing me, guys?"

"Yeah," said Huff's gang. "He's dissing you bad."

"No, I'm not. Really, I'm not." I stammered.

The zit on the end of his nose seemed to glow

at me.

I turned away so I wouldn't be looking at Huff's face. I started messing with the locker combination again.

"And what are you trying to do, breaking into my locker?" Huff growled.

He hovered over me and it was like an eclipse of the sun when it gets dark in the middle of the day.

"Oh, is this your locker?" I said in a tiny little voice I never heard before. "I didn't know that. Sorry. I musta got the wrong locker. I'm new."

I pulled my hand away from the locker like the lock had turned red hot.

I stepped away from the locker and tried to smile at Huff without looking directly at him.

"You're new now, but not for long," Huff said, wiping his nose with the cuff of his shirt sleeve. "When I get done with you, punk, you're going to be used and abused."

He gave me a shove in the chest with his hand. My books went flying.

I was stooping down to pick them up when the bell rang. All the kids who were standing around waiting for me to get beat up headed for their class-rooms.

Huff brushed by me, towing his gang behind him.

He looked down at me. I was crouched over my books, which were sprawled on the hallway floor.

"I like your shoes," he said.

Oh no. Here we go again.

Chapter Two

I always wear the coolest clothes way before anybody else.

My mom says appearance is important. She says you never get a second chance to make a first impression.

Mom reads a lot of magazines when she gets her hair done which is like twice a week so she knows all about what's in and what's out.

So I'm like always wearing stuff nobody else is wearing.

By the time they start wearing what I'm wearing, I'm wearing something else or moving to a new school.

I wore big baggy pants that slid down my hips and showed lots of my underwear long before anybody else did. Everybody made fun of me.

Now it's cool, and I'm not.

I always have the newest basketball shoes even if they cost $150.

At least I do until somebody pushes me down and sits on my back while ripping the shoes off my feet.

Heck, I'd give them the shoes if they'd just ask me. But they never do.

They just beat me up and take my shoes.

"Oh, don't cry, Lucas, dear," my mom says. "We'll buy you another pair of shoes. It's nothing to get upset about."

That's easy for her to say.

"You should feel sorry for the bullies," Mom says. "They probably come from a less fortunate family. They probably can't afford to buy their own shoes. You are lucky your father makes a lot of money."

Yep. That's me. Just call me Lucky. Lucky Luke.

"Luke! Lucas Lytle!"

When I heard Miss Swimmer's voice, I realized I had been staring at my shoes.

I wear a size seven, which is big for a kid my age. It's as if none of my body parts fit my body. My feet are too big.

They always trip me up when I try to run.

My ears are big, too. They stick out. I look really goofy in a baseball cap.

My hands are small — too small to catch a basketball without dropping it.

I have blue eyes, but when I look at myself in the mirror, one eye looks as if it's higher than the other. They don't exactly match.

My legs are too short and my arms are too long.

My nose doesn't belong to my face at all. It kind of turns up at the end, like a ski jump.

"Lucas!" said Miss Swimmer. "Lucas Lytle, are you listening to me?"

I looked up from my big feet and Miss Swimmer was standing by the blackboard (which is really green, not black. I've never seen a blackboard that was black. They're always green, but they always call them blackboards. I don't get it.)

"Yes, Miss Swimmer," I said.

"Then what was I talking about?" she said.

Miss Swimmer is a nice teacher, as far as

teachers go. She is sort of young. Younger than my mom.

She has blond hair. All her dresses have flowers on them.

"I . . . I . . . " I stammered. "I don't remember."

"Then you weren't listening, were you, Luke?" said Miss Swimmer.

All the other kids were staring at me. I could feel my big ears start to turn red.

The girl sitting in the next row was smiling at me, but it was not a friendly smile. It was more of a smirk.

She thinks I'm a doofus.

"No, Miss Swimmer. I guess I wasn't," I said.

I heard the girl in the next row laugh. It was not a nice laugh.

My ears felt as if they were on fire.

"Maybe you had better start paying attention then. You're already behind the others. I don't know what the school was like where you came from, but this class doesn't have time for foolishness. Now open your book to page 92 and read the math question aloud."

I opened the book and read without listening to what I was saying or understanding what I was reading.

I heard somebody in the back of the room hiss, "What a dope."

I glanced across the aisle and the girl sitting next to me stuck her tongue out at me.

The bell rang for lunch and we all snapped our books closed.

As I walked past Miss Swimmer, she grabbed me by the shoulder.

"You might want to talk to your parents about getting a tutor so you can catch up with the class," she said.

There is nobody like a teacher to make you feel stupid.

"I can't hold the class back just for you," Miss Swimmer said. "We have a lot of material to cover this year. Tell your parents to call me. I can recommend a tutor."

"Yes, Miss Swimmer," I said.

In the hallway I decided I hated Miss Swimmer.

She is not a nice teacher at all. She is just like all the others.

What do you have to do to become a teacher, take a meanness test?

I headed for the lunch room, my big feet in my $150 basketball shoes dragging along the floor.

I can't remember a time when I didn't feel I was all alone, even in a school with as many kids as this.

I am always being pushed and shoved by kids in a hurry to eat and it's like nobody even sees me. Like I'm invisible or something.

If I'm noticed at all, it's because my ears stick out.

Chapter Three

At lunch, we had mystery meat and instant mashed potatoes. I hate instant mashed potatoes. They taste like paste.

I have never eaten paste, but I know kids who have. They say it tastes like instant mashed potatoes.

I always sit by myself at the end of a long table.

At the other end, separated from me by four seats, are the nerds.

There's a fat kid they call Muddy.

And a geeky kid with black-rimmed glasses. I don't know his name.

And a skinny girl with her hair in braids and braces on her teeth.

She's friends with a fat girl named Wanda. Wanda the Whale.

And there's a tall kid who looks stupid, but is

actually the smartest kid in school.

The nerds ignore me. Which is better than the cool kids who all sit together at one table a couple of rows down from me.

Jason and Heather — they, like, go together. He's the best athlete in the school.

Jason plays quarterback on the football team, pitcher on the baseball team and point guard on the basketball team. He's going to be the first three-sport athlete in the pros when he grows up.

Heather is the class president and head of the pep squad. She's the one who is always at the microphone if we have an assembly or a pep rally or something.

I think she is beautiful. So does she.

Heather is always combing her hair. It's red and long and shiny.

The rest of the group, Greg and Marcie and Brandi and Dylan and Peter and Wynonna, they're all on the football team and pep squads.

Cool kids always come in pairs.

They're rude to everybody, not just me, but they especially like to pick on me.

I was minding my own business, cutting my mystery meat into chunks, when I heard the kids at the cool kids table laughing.

I looked up to see what was so funny in time to take a glob of mashed potatoes in the face. Splat!

It hit me in the forehead and slid down my nose.

Everybody was laughing at me, even the nerds at the end of the table. They wouldn't think it was so funny if it happened to them.

Wanda laughed so hard milk came out her nose.

I wiped the potatoes from my face and flicked the mess on the floor.

I lowered my head and stabbed a chunk of mystery meat with my fork. Somebody tossed a roll from across the room. It hit me in the shoulder and bounced on the floor.

I didn't look up. I just kept chewing. More rolls came flying through the air, landing in my plate, hitting me in the head, bouncing off my arms.

Everybody in the cafeteria was laughing at me. All the pretty girls, and the ugly ones too, were laughing at me.

Fight back, Dad says. Even if you lose, the other kids will respect you if you defend yourself. That's what he says.

But a roll hurts a lot less than a fist in the mouth.

Besides, what was the use? I was the new kid at school and this was my curse.

But someday . . . someday they would all be sorry.

Chapter Four

P.E. is my worst class. I'm always the last one picked when they choose teams.

I can run fast, but my feet trip me up. I end up sprawled on the ground with dirt in my face. And all the guys on my team groan.

They blame it on me when we lose.

I'm real bad at pushups. My arms are skinny and it's hard to make them lift and lower my body more than three times.

Sit-ups are not any easier. I pull and strain until it feels as if my head is going to explode. But my body just won't bend and fold like it's supposed to.

"Lytle, what is your problem, boy?" said Coach Collins. "I've seen girls — I've seen *fat* girls — do more sit-ups than you. Ain't you had your Wheaties today, boy?"

Coach is this guy with short hair and a neck as

thick as his head.

He wears his T-shirt two sizes too small to make his muscles stick out. A silver whistle hangs around his neck.

"Five more sit-ups, Lytle, you little sissy. My 80-year-old grandmother can do five sit-ups," Coach said. "You're not leaving this gym until I get five more sit-ups out of you. Do you hear me Lytle?"

"Yes, sir."

"What?"

"I said, yes, sir."

"I can't hear you, Lytle."

Coach was in the Marines. He thinks he still is.

"YES, SIR!"

I grunted. I strained. My hands felt sweaty and slippery locked behind my head.

I bent to touch my elbows to my knees. One.

I fell back on my back and breathed heavy for a few seconds. The other kids were playing basketball and dodge ball.

"LYTLE! Get busy!" Coach yelled at me.

I locked my fingers behind my head and started grunting again. Gravity has something against me.

Coach hates my guts.

"Two, that's two, Lytle. Three more."

It seemed like it took me forever to finish those five sit-ups. By the time I was done, the gym was empty.

I looked at the clock and I was already late for my next class.

"Okay, Lytle, hit the showers. You are the sorriest piece of flesh I have ever seen. But we'll fix that, Lytle. I'll make a man outta you yet. Believe me, I will. Even if it kills you."

I hurried through the double doors to the locker room.

In some ways I was glad the other guys were already showered and gone. They are always snapping towels at me when I'm undressing.

That's the other thing. I do not like people to see me naked.

I know artists think the human body is beautiful. That's why they are always painting pictures and making statues of people without any clothes on.

But my body is ugly. I'm bony where I shouldn't be and thick where I should be thin. I kind of look like I was made with the spare parts from a bunch of different people.

It's as if my body belongs to someone else. It's always tripping me up and embarrassing me. My body is my worst enemy.

I was so late for class I did not even bother to shower. I just headed straight for my locker to change out of my gym clothes.

I was in such a hurry it took me three tries to get the combination lock to work. I yanked on the lock and tossed the door open with a clang.

Oh no! I could not believe it. My locker was empty.

Somebody stole all my clothes!

I wanted to cry. I wanted to cry so bad.

But I was more afraid of Coach seeing me cry. He'd call me a baby. I could picture his face. Looking down at me. Smirking.

"What's the matter, Lytle," he would say. "Somebody take your pacifier?"

I grabbed my book bag and ran out the back door. I ran across the baseball field faster than I've ever run before.

Tears started to seep from my eyes. My heart was pounding and my ears were on fire.

I'm never going back there, I said to myself. I hate this school. I hate Coach and Miss Swimmer and all those mean, nasty kids.

I ran past the front of the school. I ran so fast that if Mr. Peterson, the principal, had looked out the window of his second-story office, he wouldn't have seen me.

He would only have seen a blur in $150 shoes streaking down the street.

I glanced up at his office, just to see if he was watching me, and my eye caught the flag flying on the flagpole. I could not believe my eyes!

There, flapping below the flag, I saw my underwear. And my socks. My shirt. My pants.

I stopped running. I stood there, staring at my clothes, my underwear, hoisted to the top of the flagpole for all the world to see.

I felt something well up inside me. It wasn't tears. It wasn't shame.

It was something I had never felt before.

I felt a fury inside me. A rage. A hard tight ball

of anger lodged like a stone in my chest.

I've gotten mad before. I know how that feels. It kind of flashes inside your head and then goes away.

You get mad and then you get over it.

This was different. I knew this was something that would not go away.

Not ever.

And it scared me.

Chapter Five

"Lucas! Lucas, honey, wake up. You'll be late for school."

I groaned and pulled the pillow over my head.

"Luke! You heard me. Get up. Get up right now," Mom said.

She yanked the pillow from my head.

"I don't feel good," I said, using my best raspy voice.

"Nonsense," she said. "You're fine. Now hurry up and get dressed. You'll miss the bus."

I coughed and retched a couple of times.

"I better go see a doctor," I said in the voice of the half-dead. "I think I have cancer."

Mom ripped the covers off my bed. She was trying not to laugh.

"Now you're being silly," she said. "Really, Lucas, I don't have time for this. I need to get to work and you need to catch that school bus."

"I'm serious, Mom," I pleaded. "I really feel sick. You'll be sorry if I go to school. I'll puke and they'll call you at work to come and get me."

"I'll chance it," she said, and I could see she was not fooling around.

I swung my legs off the bed onto the wood floor of my bedroom.

I like my room. It's got my posters on the wall, comic books on the floor, my Nintendo, and a color TV with remote control. I could stay in my room all my life and I'd be happy.

But that won't happen. I have to go to school and be miserable.

I was faking before, but now I really did feel sick as I pulled on a pair of jeans and a shirt, some socks and my $150 basketball shoes.

I grabbed my book bag and slung it over my shoulder. Skipping the juice and bowl of cereal Mom left on the table, I left the house without saying good bye.

They'll miss me when I'm dead, I thought as I walked down the sidewalk.

I waited by myself at the school bus stop while the other kids pushed and chased each other around. A couple of the older boys stood behind a tree smoking cigarettes.

I was kind of hoping somebody would grab my book bag and make me chase them.

I wanted one of the older guys to offer me a smoke, even if it meant I would really get cancer and die.

But nobody did. They just acted as if I wasn't there.

That's the curse of being a new kid.

The bus came and we all got on. It was crowded and some kids had to sit three to a seat. I sat by myself. Nobody wanted to sit next to me.

Every time a kid passed me toward the back of the bus, they would slap me on the head. One kid, Billy, slapped me so hard my head cracked against the metal bar on the seat in front of me.

"Hey!" I said, "Cut that out!"

"Hey," mimicked Billy in a sissy voice. "Cut that out."

Everybody in the bus started laughing. They all

started saying, "Hey, cut that out. Hey, cut that out."

I felt that strange feeling inside my stomach again. I turned my head away and looked out the school bus window.

Billy always sits way in the back of the bus. He is one of the kids who smokes before the bus comes. He sits in the back with three of his buddies.

The bus rocked and bounced until the brakes squeaked and jolted us to a stop in front of the school. The bus driver pulled the lever and the doors folded open.

Kids pushed and shoved each other in the aisle on the way out. I got out of my seat in a hurry before Billy and his friends could slap me on the head again.

I jumped off the bus. Billy was right behind me.

I was headed to the front door when I heard Billy howl.

It was a horrifying sound.

Chapter Six

I swung around and saw that Billy's arm was caught in the school bus door.

"Help me! Help me!" he was yelling.

His eyes were red and his face was contorted in pain.

"Aaaaghhhh!" he screamed as he tried to pull his arm from the bus door. Tears were flowing down his face. "My arm! My arm!"

He looked like an animal caught in a hunter's trap. Sometimes when an animal is caught in a trap, it will chew its leg off to get free.

I was waiting for somebody to show up and cut off Billy's arm when the bus door popped open.

Billy fell flat on the ground. He was clutching his arm with his hand and rolling around in pain on the asphalt.

Everybody in the school was staring at him

thrashing on the ground. A couple of his friends lifted him up and started carrying him to the school nurse.

His arm hung from his body like some useless rag. I was sure he must have broken it in a couple of places.

I started to turn toward the school when I looked up and saw the face of the school bus driver through the open doors. I don't think I ever looked at the driver before.

When I did, I gasped.

The bus driver was looking straight at me. There was a monstrous grin on her face.

She nodded to me and closed the doors.

I felt that strange feeling stir in my stomach.

I was late getting to Miss Swimmer's class. I had my head down, headed to my desk, when one of the kids in my row stuck out his foot.

I fell flat on my face.

"Have a nice trip?" he said.

The whole class started laughing.

"Class. Class," said Miss Swimmer. "That's not funny. Leon, keep your feet under your desk from now on."

I slipped my book bag from my shoulders and sat down at my desk.

I looked across the aisle. The girl next to me was twisting her hair around her finger.

She had very curly hair.

I turned my head away and stared at the back of Leon's head.

He made me so mad. And Miss Swimmer didn't even punish him for tripping me.

I hated her more and more every day.

I can't remember anything we learned in class that day. It was a miserable day.

The bell rang and we all got up to leave.

I was right behind Leon so I saw it all. It looked as if it happened in slow motion.

He was walking past Miss Swimmer when he stepped on one of his shoe laces and tripped. He put his hand out to brace his fall, but his head hit the corner of Miss Swimmer's desk.

Leon never ties his shoes.

Kids heard his head crack all the way in the hall.

It opened a gash over his left eye. Blood was

squirting in the air before his head hit the floor.

He was sprawled across the floor. He didn't move or moan or anything. A red pool spread from his head.

I figured he was dead for sure.

Some girl screamed when she saw the blood.

"I didn't touch him, Miss Swimmer," I said.

"I know that, Lucas," she said, kneeling beside the fallen boy. "It's not your fault."

But I wish it was. I wish I had busted Leon's head open myself.

I felt bad about thinking thoughts like that. I'm not like that. Really, I'm not.

At the door, I turned to look back at Leon. And what I saw sent shivers down my neck.

Miss Swimmer was still kneeling beside Leon, but she was looking right at me. Her face was hideous.

The lips of her mouth were pulled away from her teeth in the same ghastly grin as I had seen on the face of the bus driver.

Chapter Seven

Everybody in the lunch room was talking about what happened to Billy and Leon.

"Two kids in the hospital on the same day. That's gotta be a record," said Muddy.

"Yeah, and it couldn't have happened to two nicer guys than Billy Butkis and Leon Lennon," said Arnold, the geeky kid with thick black-framed glasses.

Arnold bit into his mystery meat on a bun and chewed it like a cow eating grass. I saw him look over at me and I quickly looked away.

"What are you looking at, Lytle?" he said with his mouth full. You could see the mushy gray meat in his mouth while he talked.

I ignored him and sipped on the straw in my box of milk. Getting picked on by bullies is bad enough. I don't need nerds messing with me.

"Are you ignoring me, Lytle?" he said.

I'm trying to, I thought to myself. I'm trying to very hard.

I was starting to feel that tingly feeling in my stomach. But I kept my face down and minded my own business.

I was raising my sandwich to my mouth when I felt him standing behind me.

"Hey Puke," said Arnold. "That's your name isn't it? Puke Lytle?"

I turned my head and his face was inches from my own. He has very thick glasses and it makes his watery brown eyes look enormous.

The other nerds were watching us. Wanda started to giggle, and milk squirted out of her mouth.

"Look," I said, feeling my stomach churning, "why don't you just go back to your friends and leave me alone. I wasn't bothering you."

Arnold pushed his glasses up his nose and sneered at me.

"But you do bother me, Puke. You think you're better than us. I see it in your face."

"I don't think I'm better than you," I said.

"Sure you do," Arnold said, picking up a

French fry from my plate. "Everybody thinks they're better than us. You're no different."

I felt my face start to burn. The churning in my stomach was starting to make me sick. Why was this happening to me?

"Why don't you just back off, Arnold," I said, but I didn't recognize my voice. It was as if somebody else was talking for me.

"You're no different from the others," repeated Arnold, "except that you have a French fry coming out of your ear."

And he jammed the French fry in my ear.

Everybody at his end of the table was laughing. I took a swing at him and missed.

Arnold went back to his seat and slapped high-fives with the other nerds.

I guess no matter how far down you are, you can always feel big if there is somebody below you.

I could feel the anger inside my gut. It felt as if my stomach was eating me from the inside out. I thought I was going to get sick.

But then I heard Arnold cry out.

"Oh, God! Ow, ow, ow!" he screamed,

clutching his stomach.

"What's wrong? What's the matter?" said Bruce, the stupid-looking genius kid.

"My stomach! The pain! I can't stand it!" yelled Arnold.

The whole lunch room went quiet. Arnold's screams echoed off the walls of the cafeteria.

His friends looked horrified. We all watched helplessly as he suddenly slammed headfirst into the table.

His head hit his lunch tray and food went flying all over. I saw blood on his head.

But it turned out to be ketchup.

He started going into convulsions and making these horrible retching sounds.

Then just as suddenly as he fell forward, he shot back up in his chair.

His mouth opened, but no words came out. His eyes looked as if they were going to pop out of his head.

"Arnold! What's happening to you?" yelled Wanda.

Arnold made a gurgling sound and then a vile

stream of green puke spewed from his mouth. It flew across the table and hit Wanda splat in the face.

Then she started gagging and retching. Pretty soon the same green stream of slime shot from her face.

Before you knew it, all the nerds were clutching their stomachs. They started moaning and screaming. Their eyes popped wide open. Their mouths filled with green puke and they threw up all over the cafeteria.

It was pretty disgusting.

Every kid in the lunch room, including me, left their food on their trays uneaten and ran for the doors.

I saw a few kids get sick and throw up on the floor. Other kids stepped in it, slipped and fell. Then the ones who fell got sick themselves.

The whole cafeteria was one stinking, slimy pile of puke-covered kids.

I was trying hard not to get sick myself as I ran past the lunch counter. Out of the corner of my eye I saw the lady in the plastic hairnet who slaps the food on the trays.

What I saw made my stomach roll over. I had

to gulp to keep from losing my lunch.

The lunch lady's face distorted by that same horrible grin. She waved her slop spoon at me.

I ran into the hall screaming.

Chapter Eight

There was hardly anybody in gym class because so many kids had been sent home sick or to the hospital with stomach pains.

I thought maybe Coach Collins would take it easy on us because there is not much you can do in P.E. with only six kids.

Boy was I wrong.

He seemed mad at us that everybody else was gone.

"Okay, listen up. So a bunch of sissies lost their cookies in the lunchroom. That don't mean the rest of you are gonna get a free ride from me, see," Coach Collins said.

He walked back and forth in front of us with his hands clasped behind his back. His whistle glistened in the lights of the gymnasium.

"I smell something fishy. I think some wise

guys figured they could skip phys ed if they just pretended they got the flu. Well, it ain't gonna work."

I looked at the kid standing next to me. His name was Ralph. He was a short little round guy with spiked red hair. He hated gym as much as I did.

Ralph looked back at me, and sort of shrugged his shoulders.

"Okay, you two," snapped Coach Collins, pointing his finger at us. "Yes, you. Step forward."

Ralph and I gulped and took one step forward. The other four guys took one step back, as if they were getting ready to turn and run.

We had all seen Coach Collins like this before. It is not a pretty sight. Usually he gets this way after his basketball team blows a big lead and loses the game.

His face gets all red. The nostrils of his nose flare wide. And the short hairs on his head look like a thousand little pins.

"Lytle. Buchmann."

"Yes, Coach," Ralph and I answered together.

"See those ropes?"

We looked where he was pointing. There were

two ropes tied to the rafters of the gymnasium. The ropes were at least 20 feet long.

"Those ropes, sir?" I said.

"Those ropes, sir?" Coach Collins said, mimicking me. "Yes, you dunce. Those ropes. They're the only ropes in the gym."

I knew what was coming. My stomach started hurting again.

"I want you two to climb those ropes. I want you to climb them fast. The first one to touch the rafter and slide back down is done for the day and gets an A for the class. The loser . . . " he paused and sneered at each of us individually. "Well, let's just say you don't want to be the loser. Okay, GO!"

Against our will, Ralph and I raced each other to the ropes.

Ralph is heavier than me and it should have been easy for me to beat him to the top. But I have really weak arms and it's hard for me to pull myself up.

As much as I hate sit-ups, I hate climbing that rope even worse.

I wrapped the rope around my ankles like Coach Collins taught us. I put one hand over the other and started trying to pull myself up the rope.

Beside me I could hear Ralph grunt and gasp.

"Let's go, Lytle, you worm. Don't let that fat little dough boy show you up," yelled Coach Collins.

"Go Ralph! You can do it! Beat the new kid!" the other boys shouted.

That made me mad. I put one hand over the other, one after the other, and lifted myself up the rope.

"Buchmann, you lard-butt. You can do better than that!" said Coach Collins. "Don't let that noodle-armed wimp beat you!"

The other kids were getting really excited.

"Go Ralph go!"

"Don't let Pukey Lukey beat you!"

"You can do it, Ralph!"

"Pull harder, Ralph!"

My heart was pounding. Sweat was stinging my eyes. The rope was rough and scratchy in my hands.

I looked down and I could see the upturned faces of the kids below. I could hear Ralph's heavy breathing and animal grunts as he pulled up beside me.

I looked at his face. It was red and splotchy. His hair was matted to his face.

I looked at him and I saw him look back at me.

And I could see that he hated me.

And I knew I hated him too.

I hated Ralph. I hated Coach Collins. I hated all the kids down below yelling for me to lose.

I felt that hardness inside my stomach, like the knot of rope tied above my head.

My anger pulled me up that rope.

I could still hear the kids yelling below, but they seemed so far away. They looked tiny beneath me.

"Ralph! He's beating you!"

"Harder, Ralph, pull harder!"

"You're a pitiful pile of pig flesh, Buchmann. I ought to cut you up and fry you with my eggs!" bellowed Coach Collins.

I thought I had Ralph beat. But with some burst of super-human strength, Ralph Buchmann huffed and puffed and pulled himself to the top of the rope. I saw him reach for the rafter.

I knew I had lost. I had lost to a little round fat

kid. I hated myself, but I hated Ralph even more.

And then I don't know what happened. I heard the kids down below gasp.

Maybe his hands slipped. Maybe he was just too tired to hold on.

But like a bomb from the clouds, Ralph Buchmann fell to earth.

I heard him scream as he went down.

"Ahhhhhhhhiiiiieeeeeeeee!"

He fell head first. His arms were straight out in front of him, like a dive-bombing Superman.

He almost looked as if he was trying to aim himself. I think he was getting ready to die.

From that height, he would have killed himself, except that he scored a perfect bull's-eye right on top of Coach Collins.

"He's dead!" one of the kids shouted.

"Ralph killed the Coach!" another kid said.

"They're both dead!"

I slid down the rope so fast I burned my hands.

When I reached the floor, I saw Ralph and Coach Collins tangled together in a motionless heap. It was hard to tell which body parts belonged to Ralph and which belonged to Coach Collins.

Neither was breathing.

I could not believe this had happened. Not even after all the other bizarre things that had gone on today. Broken arms and mass vomiting. That's one thing. But people getting killed, this was too much. This was a massacre.

I didn't get it.

What's going on? I thought. Why is this happening?

Then I saw the look on Ralph's face.

<u>Chapter Nine</u>

The graveyard is dark. A full moon shines through the dead branches of the trees. It's cold and windy.

I am standing by myself, shivering. I forgot to wear my jacket and the wind rips through my T-shirt.

The other kids from school huddle together beside the open grave.

A woman in black weeps loudly.

"Oh my God, my God," she cries. "Why have you done this to me?"

The agony in her voice chills me from the inside the same way the cold wind gives me shivers on the outside.

I feel something creeping up behind me. But I am too cold to care.

A clammy hand clamps on my shoulder. The hand is strong, but bony.

A deep dark voice whispers in my ear. "It's your fault. You killed him."

I swing around to face my accuser.

There is nobody there.

I feel a tremor shoot though my body like a jolt of electricity. This is really weird.

This place gives me the creeps.

The hearse arrives and they pull the coffin out the back door. It's a small casket like the ones for babies.

It only takes two kids to carry it, one on each end as if they were moving a table.

The woman's sobs grow louder.

"My baby, my baby. They've taken my baby from me!" she cries.

The wind picks up and blows through the dead trees. A cloud passes over the moon. The graveyard is so dark I can hardly see.

I hear the voice again. It's coming from the trees.

"You killed him. You killed him. You killed him."

I clamp my hands over my ears. But I can still

hear the voice.

"You'll burn in hell. You'll burn."

They bring the casket to the mother and lay it at her feet.

She holds her face in her hands so I can't see who she is. Her body, dressed all in black, shakes with sobs. A man puts his hands on her shoulders and tries to comfort her.

"They murdered my baby!" the woman shrieks.

It's so cold outside. I feel as if I'm being frozen to death. Why didn't I bring my jacket?

The minister steps beside the coffin. He is a tall, thin man with a pale face. He holds a Bible in his bony hands.

I hear the voice. It feels as if it's almost inside me.

"You killed him. You'll burn forever in eternal damnation."

"I didn't mean to!" I scream.

Everybody turns to look at me.

Ashamed, I look down at the ground. I stare at the leaves blowing past my feet as the minister begins to talk.

"Something terrible has visited our small community. I don't know what it is. Perhaps we are paying with the lives of our children for our own sins. Our selfishness. Our greed. Our jealousy."

I look up. All heads are bowed, all hands are clasped. I can't see their faces but I recognize some of the kids.

I see Wanda and Bruce. Greg, Dylan and Pete. I recognize the shape and attitude of Huff. Mr. Peterson, the principal, is standing beside the mother. Miss Swimmer is there too.

"Whatever it is," the minister says, "this demon in our midst is a curse on our community that has come from somewhere else. This is something new, something foreign, that has besieged us. It has moved in among us. Its hunger for misery, sickness and death will not be satisfied until it has destroyed us. Or until we have destroyed it first."

A sudden gust of wind blows across the graveyard. It makes the tree limbs creak and groan. Dust blows in my face and stings my eyes. I turn my back to the wind and I hear the voice again.

"You will die. We will murder your body. We

will burn your soul."

I don't want to die. I didn't mean to hurt anyone.

I approach the crowd gathered around the casket. I want them to know that I mean no harm.

They lower the casket into the grave. The mother throws a rose on top of the casket, then collapses to the ground. Her shrieks drown out the howling of the wind.

I start to say something but no words come out. I step closer to the grave and look down on the casket.

Suddenly the lid pops open.

I am staring at the dead face of Ralph Buchmann. His eyes are wide open, staring back at me.

His face is frozen in that horrible grin. He is laughing at me from his grave.

I step back in horror and stumble.

The mourners turn toward me as if noticing me for the first time. Together, they move toward me like a mob.

"You killed him," they say. "You murdered

Ralph. You are the one. You must die."

The mother lifts the black veil from her face. Her lips are stretched in that ghastly grin.

I turn to the minister for help and gasp. His face has the same awful grin.

They all do. Mr. Peterson, Miss Swimmer, Huff and Arnold, Greg and Dylan.

The cloud moves away from the moon. The graveyard is illuminated as if by a spot light. I can see all their faces, glowing with that terrifying grin. It's the grin of vengeance.

"You must die. You must die," they say, moving toward me. "You murdered Ralph. You must die."

I turn to run and they start to chase me.

I stumble through the graveyard. Tombstones pop up to stop me. Behind me I can hear the footsteps of the mob.

I dodge the tombstones, weaving my way through the cemetery. I hear myself crying. I hear the voices of the mob.

"Burn his soul! Rot in hell! Kill him, kill him. Kill the new kid."

I see the street beyond the edge of the cemetery. It's lit up by street lights. I'll be safe if I can reach the street.

I am shivering on the outside, but my lungs are burning up inside. My legs are heavy. I am too tired to keep going.

The footsteps behind me grow louder.

I look over my shoulder and see the moon through the trees. The moon itself is grinning at me.

"Agggghhhhhh!"

I try to run faster. They will kill me if I don't keep going.

I am close to the edge of the cemetery when a hand reaches out from the grave and grabs my ankle. I fall to the ground, thrashing and screaming.

"Let go, let go, let go of me!"

The hand will not let go.

The mob is upon me. Their hideous grinning faces bend toward me. Their hands reach for my face to pull my hair and rip out my eyes.

I know I'm going to die.

Chapter Ten

My own screams woke me up.

I lay there, breathing hard, sweating. My heart pounded in my chest like an angry man trying to get out.

That was no dream. That was too real.

It wasn't yet light out. It was too early to get up. But I was too scared to go back to sleep. I just lay stiffly on my back in the bed and stared at the shadows on the ceiling.

I tried to figure it all out. This was way too weird.

I wish I had a brother. A big brother. He would know what to do.

Or two bigger brothers. Or four. And all of them bigger than Huff and Billy and Leon all put together. They would protect me.

We would be the Fighting Lytle Brothers. That

would be great.

But I don't have any brothers. I'm an only child.

It's lonely being an only child. You get your own room, but that's about it.

When you have brothers and sisters, you can gang up on your parents. But when you're an only child, you're always outnumbered by adults.

If I had brothers and sisters, I would have somebody to talk to.

You can't really talk to your Dad about this stuff. My dad, he only knows how it used to be when he was a kid. It's not like that any more.

"Anybody gives you a hard time, Luke, you just tell the teacher," Dad says.

He wouldn't last a day in my world.

And Mom! Forget it. She like gets too excited about everything. Everything turns into a big deal. Sometimes she just goes nuts about the dumbest things.

"Lucas! Who left this mess in the living room? Look at all this trash. Candy wrappers, drink cups. ARE YOU LISTENING TO ME!!!!!"

Kill me now.

So when you really *do* have a big deal, like when nobody in the school likes you and you've got crazy grinning guys crawling into your dreams, you do not want her to flip out.

I guessed I was alone on this one. Just like always.

I slid out of bed and into a pair of jeans.

Mom was in the kitchen making breakfast. Dad was reading the paper.

"Good morning, Lukey. Give Mommy a kiss," Mom said. "Do you want eggs for breakfast? Eggs and toast?"

Dad looked up from his paper.

"What's the name of your school?" he asked.

"JFK Junior," I said.

I gave mom a kiss. I kind of needed a hug, too. But then Mom said, "When was the last time you washed your face?"

"Is that John F. Kennedy Middle School?" Dad asked.

"Oh, Larry, don't you know the name of your child's school?" Mom said.

"Know his school? Heck, I can hardly remember what city I live in," said Dad. "This is Pittsburgh, isn't it?"

"If you were home a little more, you might not get moved around as much," Mom said. "You might learn what grade your son is in."

"I want scrambled eggs," I said.

Dad shook the paper and buried his nose in its pages again. From behind the newspaper, he said, "There's a story in today's paper about some strange string of accidents at John F. Kennedy Middle School."

I gulped. He's going to find out about Ralph. And Coach Collins.

Or did I dream that, too?

He didn't look up from the paper.

"Do you know anything about this, Luke?" he said as if he was talking to the business page.

This was my chance to tell my folks about all the weird stuff that had been going on. Maybe they'd know what to do. Maybe this kind of thing happened to them, too, when they were kids.

I looked at Mom. I looked at Dad.

Naw.

"What stuff?" I said. I put on my dumb face. "I don't know anything about anything strange going on."

But inside I was pretty scared. Maybe I *had* killed them.

"Um, so, like, what's the story say?" I said. "Somebody get hurt or something?"

Dad shuffled the pages without looking up.

"Some kids in the hospital. Food poisoning, they think. Also, there's one kid with a broken arm, and another with a cracked skull. Freak accidents, the principal says."

"That's it?" I said.

Maybe Ralph was all in my imagination.

"And there's a kid in a coma and a gym teacher they think might be paralyzed from the neck down. Some sort of accident involving a rope," Dad said. He lowered his paper and sipped from his coffee cup. "Sounds like a lawsuit to me."

"Here, honey," said Mom. "Scrambled eggs and toast."

She set the plate on the breakfast bar. I slipped

onto the stool. I squirted catsup on my eggs (I like them that way) and grabbed my fork.

"Aagggg!" I gasped when I saw my eggs. The fork fell from my hands. It clanked on the tile kitchen floor.

Staring at me from the plate were the scrambled brains and bloody face of Ralph.

Chapter Eleven

I was at my locker, trying to get the lock to work. The bell was about to ring.

"Hey, Bad News," said a voice so vile it could only belong to Huff.

I looked up from my lock. I studied his face for a minute.

Boy, I'd hate to meet Huff's parents. They must be double ugly to make something that creepy.

He wiped a sleeve across his nose and spit on the hallway floor.

"Yes, I'm talking to you, Puke. You, Bad News. Seems everywhere you go, bad things just tag along," Huff said.

"Yeah," I said, "and you better watch out. It might be contagious."

I don't know what made me say that. A death wish of some kind.

"Ooooo," said Huff, stepping back in fake fear. He turned his head to the gang of guys behind him. "Look out, boys. Something bad might happen to us."

"We're scared," they said.

"We're trembling," they said.

"He might hurt us," they said.

"I might trip and bump my head," Huff said in a whiny voice. "Or my tummy might not feel good."

I turned away and went back to trying to open my locker. I had enough trouble.

"Here," Huff said, turning his voice as soft and sweet as cotton candy. "Let us help you with your locker. You seem to be having some trouble there, Bad News."

He shoved me to the floor and started kicking the heck out of my locker.

"Hey!" I said, but one of his gang held me down to the floor with a boot on my chest.

Huff must wear boots with steel toes because he kicked the heck out of that locker door. Just pounded it.

The door collapsed beneath his black boots. It crumpled in on itself and wedged solid inside the locker.

I kept thinking, where are all the teachers? Don't they hear the racket he's making kicking that locker? Where's Principal Peterson?

How come I'm always alone?

Then Huff spun on the heels of his boots and turned toward me.

The guy with his foot on my chest stepped on my head, holding it down.

I was pinned to the floor. I could see his feet in those big black boots coming at me.

I saw him stop in front of my face. The toes of his boots were aimed at my nose. He pulled his leg back.

I watched his boot come at my face like my head was a soccer ball.

He stopped his kick just inches from my face. He laughed. His whole gang laughed. Their laughter echoed off the empty hallway walls.

I never screamed. I never said a word.

But I wet my pants.

"See guys," Huff said, turning away and walking down the hall. "He's not so bad. He's just a little baby who needs his diaper changed."

Inside my stomach, I felt the knot tighten. The ball of anger grew larger.

Something inside me slipped a little further away from my control.

Chapter Twelve

I sat with my hands over my lap outside Principal Peterson's office. I have never been so embarrassed. I have never felt so mad.

Somebody will pay for this. Somebody will be sorry.

"Please step in here, Luke," said Miss Smathers, Mr. Peterson's secretary.

I stood up, but kept my hands folded over the wet spot on my pants.

Oh, I'm a lucky guy, all right: Some bully makes me pee my pants and I'm the one who gets in trouble.

I'm cursed, that's what I am. The Curse of the New Kid.

I walked into the principal's office with my head down. My eyes were locked on the floor. I didn't look up, even after I sat down in a chair in front of his desk.

"Well," said Mr. Peterson, sitting behind his desk. "I see you've had a little . . . accident."

I looked up from my lap.

Mr. Peterson is the kind of man all the adults think is so nice. He has a round, soft face and a semi-circle of blond hair around his head. He always wears a white shirt and tie.

He tells parents how smart their kids are, or how athletic, or talented. Even with the bad kids, he always has something nice to say.

But if you're a kid, it's a different story. We know that, inside, Mr. Peterson is a mean and nasty man.

I looked at Mr. Peterson and saw the smirk on his lips.

"Yes, a little accident, indeed," he said. He stood up from behind his desk, looked at the wet stain on my pants and sat back down. "Would you like to tell me what happened?"

No. No, I wouldn't, I thought to myself. I hate Huff, but I hate Mr. Peterson just as much. I wouldn't spit on him if he were on fire.

"Would this have anything to do with the damage to your locker?" said Mr. Peterson.

I folded my hands over my lap again, and stared at the floor.

"Well?" said Mr. Peterson, and I could hear the hardness in his voice.

I said nothing.

"Look, Lytle, you're new here. Maybe you don't know how things work around here. I'll spell it out for you. I ask a question. You answer. You got it?"

The last words had the sharpness of a dagger. They weren't a question. They were a threat.

"Yes, sir," I mumbled.

"Good. So let's have it. What bad widdow boy make Wookey Wyddle wet his pants?" said Mr. Peterson, talking to me as if I was a baby.

I hated Mr. Peterson. I hated him more than anybody in the world.

"Nobody," I said. "I was late for class and I didn't have time to go to the bathroom, and I just couldn't hold it anymore."

I kept my head down so he couldn't look into

my face.

"You're a liar," said Mr. Peterson. "Just like the rest. I'm trying to help your sorry butt, but you're just like every other smart alecky little punk at this school."

I glanced up. Mr. Peterson's face was red. The top of his bald head was just about glowing. He had spit on the corner of his mouth.

"What about your locker? What happened there?" he said, and the spittle flew from his lips.

"It's broken," I said.

"I KNOW THAT!" he screamed, jumping up from his desk. "DO YOU THINK I'M AN IDIOT!"

"The lock," I said, pushing myself back in the chair to avoid getting splattered with spit. "The lock is broken. I...I got mad and I just started kicking it."

He reached into his pants pocket and pulled out a handkerchief. He mopped his face with the hankie. When he was done, the smirk was back on his face.

"That's your story?"

"Yes, sir."

"You want me to believe a little runt like you

kicked the stuffing out of a hallway locker with his tennis shoes? I don't think soooo."

Mr. Peterson sat back down behind his desk. He pressed a button on his telephone.

"Miss Smathers, bring that pair of pants for Mr. Lytle," he said. He took his finger off the button.

"If that's the game you want to play, Luke, be my guest," he said. "But it is a game you cannot win. I will send your parents the bill for the locker. Maybe you can make up a better story for them than you did for me."

He leaned toward me, resting his weight on his forearms.

"You just made a mistake, Luke. You don't want to mess with me. From now on, I'm your worst enemy."

The door opened and Mr. Peterson leaned back in his chair. All the redness drained from his face. He looked calm and mild-mannered.

Miss Smathers handed me a pair of pants and showed me to the bathroom off Mr. Peterson's office.

"You can change in here," she said. "I'll send your soiled pants home."

I went inside the bathroom. The pants were the ugliest plaid I have ever seen. I shed mine and pulled on the ones Miss Smathers gave me. They were tight around the waist, but even worst than that they were about three inches too short on the legs.

I looked as if I had escaped from the circus. I looked like a geek, a total geek.

Chapter Thirteen

Everybody stared at me as I walked through the halls.

The crowded hallway seemed to open up as I approached. Kids stopped what they were doing to watch the New Freak In The Geeky Pants go by.

Girls snickered and giggled, whispering things to their friends. Boys shoved each other and pointed at me. Their laughs were loud and exaggerated.

I tried to ignore them. I tried to pretend I was invisible. I wished I never existed. I wished I had never been born.

"Look, it's Bozo's kid brother," somebody said.

"Naw. That's Jethro," another kid said.

"Hey, Puke, what happened? You dress in the dark this morning?"

"Hey, look, his socks don't match!"

The heat started at the top of my head in the roots of my hair. It worked its way down my forehead to my ears and past my neck. It reached my chest and my heart turned to coal.

In my stomach, I felt the heat bubble and boil. My guts were churning but I didn't feel sick. I felt the hard hot burn of total hatred for everyone and everything around me.

Up ahead, coming toward me but not seeing me, I saw Jason and Heather, arm in arm. Behind them were Greg and Marcie, Brandi and Dylan, Pete and Wynonna.

They were in their own little world, as always. The guys had that jock strut down. They walked like they had football pads on even when they were wearing shorts.

And the girls, they always looked like they knew everybody was watching them while they didn't see anybody but themselves. They made sure their hair swung when they walked.

They were the only ones in the school who had no idea I was walking around in a pair of plaid pants two sizes too small.

But not for long.

"Ewwww. What's that?" said Heather.

Jason looked up and burst out laughing. The other couples slammed to a stop behind him and everybody started giggling and snickering at me.

"I knew you had no taste, Puke, but puleeese have the decency to spare those of us who do," said Jason.

That got a big round of laughs from the whole hallway. Jason's so clever. A regular comedian.

"Why don't you shut up, you stupid jock?" I said.

I don't know what made me say something like that.

All the laughter stopped.

Somebody said, "Ooooo."

The smug look on Jason's face disappeared.

"I hope I didn't hear you right, Puke. You didn't just tell me to shut up, did you?"

"Which word didn't you understand?" I said. "Shut or up?"

A nervous giggle rippled through the crowd. The cheerleaders, Heather and Brandi and Marcie and

Wynonna, stepped away from their boyfriends. Greg, Dylan and Pete stepped up beside Jason.

There was no getting by them. And no turning back.

"You're dead meat, Puke Breath," snarled Jason.

It's funny, but for some reason I was not afraid. Maybe they were going to break every bone in my body. Maybe they were going to kill me.

But I wasn't scared.

I felt a strange serenity. As if I was ready for whatever came next.

I dropped my book bag to the floor with a thud. My fingers coiled into fists.

They all jumped me at the same time.

I felt fists hitting me in the stomach and the face. I heard bones crunch and flesh tear.

I felt the warm wet trickle of blood. I heard shouts of anger. I heard cries of pain.

But I felt nothing, nothing but the hard, hot rage inside me.

Somebody screamed. It was a horrifying scream. It startled me so much I stopped swinging my fists and kicking my feet.

I realized then I had been fighting with my eyes closed.

When I opened them, I could not believe what I saw. For the first time since the fight began, I felt sick to my stomach. I thought I might throw up.

Chapter Fourteen

Jason's face was a horrible mess of blood and ripped skin. He didn't look like someone who had been in a fight. He looked like someone whose face had been melted by a blow torch.

Dylan's hands were mangled and twisted as if they had been caught in farm machinery. It looked like every bone in his fingers was smashed.

Greg was even worse. His clothes were shredded and soaked with blood. There were claw marks across his chest. Blood spurted like there was a hole in his chest. His ribs poked through the skin.

Pete. I couldn't look at Pete. His left arm hung limply at his side as if the only thing holding it to his body was the tattered shirt he was wearing. Every bit of his clothing was ripped and slashed. The side of his face was so bloody you couldn't see one of his eyes. His lips were puffy. He coughed, and his teeth crumpled in his mouth.

I turned away from the broken, bloody and twisted bodies on the hallway floor.

Did I do this? I couldn't have.

There were four of them — all big athletic guys.

And just one of me.

I looked at the terrified faces of the kids in the hall. None of them looked at me. They all stared at Heather, Brandi, Wynonna and Marcie. Their mouths hung open and you could see they were truly frightened by what they saw.

I turned my head toward the cheerleaders.

They looked back at me with wide grins stretched across their faces. Their teeth were smeared red. Blood dripped from their long, sharp fingernails.

Chapter Fifteen

I tilted my head back and let out the loudest, cruelest laugh of my life.

I didn't understand what was going on. But I was glad it happened. Those guys deserved everything they got.

I tucked my shirt into my plaid pants. I picked up my book bag. I looked at the stunned and speechless kids standing in the hall.

A strange cackle escaped my lips.

Confused and afraid, the other kids stepped away from me as I walked down the hall to the cafeteria.

I pushed my tan plastic tray of spaghetti and salad along the lunch line rails trying to figure it all out.

It was all too confusing. None of it made any sense.

Maybe I was not cursed after all.

It sounds strange, but maybe I was being protected by some guardian angel for new kids. A guardian angel who kicked butt.

Who knew? Who cared?

All that mattered to me was that bad things were happening to bad people.

I could live with that.

I slid into my usual chair at the end of the nerds' table. I was starving.

I was so hungry I didn't notice Muddy plop his tray next to mine.

"Is this seat taken?" he said.

I looked around me to see who he was talking to. There was nobody sitting there but me.

"Are you kidding?" I said. "Nobody ever sits with me."

"But I'd like to," Muddy said. "If you don't mind, of course."

"Sure, go ahead. It's a free country. Sit wherever you want," I said, and shoveled a wad of spaghetti into my mouth.

Wanda came and sat down across from

Muddy. Before I knew it the whole nerd crowd had shifted down to my end of the table.

Must have been the pants.

"We heard what you did to the jocks," said Muddy.

"I didn't do anything," I said.

"I heard you put all four of those guys in the hospital," said Wanda.

"It wasn't me," I said.

"How'd you do it? Do you carry brass knuckles or something?" said Bruce.

I set my fork down on my tray.

"Look, I don't know what you guys think happened, but I didn't hurt any of those guys," I said.

"Then who did?" Muddy said. "There was blood all over the hallway."

"It was the cheerleaders," I said.

Milk shot out of Wanda's nose and squirted Muddy in the face.

"Get real," she snorted. "The Barbie dolls beat up the football team. Like, right."

"I don't get it either, but that's what happened," I said. I stabbed my fork into a slice of tomato.

Bruce stood up and leaned across the lunch table. He extended his hand.

"I want to apologize for giving you a hard time, Luke. Arnold feels the same way," he said.

I'm not one to hold a grudge. I shook Bruce's hand.

"Where is Arnold?" I asked.

"Um, he's still in the hospital. They don't know what's wrong. Some bad intestinal virus, they think," said Arnold.

"He can't keep anything down," Muddy added. "They have to feed him through a tube in his stomach."

"He's in the same room with Ralph," said Wanda. "Ralph's out of his coma, you know."

Whatever I was eating turned sour in my mouth. I spit it out on my plate and took a big gulp of milk to wash away the taste. That bad dream was still inside my head.

I twisted another wad of spaghetti onto my fork and shoved it in my mouth. The nerds were jabbering about Star Trek and the Internet. Boring stuff.

Then all of a sudden there was silence.

I felt somebody standing behind me. I looked up from my lunch tray and all the nerds were staring over my shoulders.

Uh-oh. This could only mean Huff.

Chapter Sixteen

I waited for a tray of spaghetti to be dumped on my head. Or my chair to be yanked out from under me. Or a big wad of spit to land on my shoulder.

When none of that happened, I opened my eyes.

Standing behind me was the girl who sits next to me in Miss Swimmer's class. Her name's Ruby. Ruby Rogers.

She's cute. Really cute.

"Um, hi, Luke," she said.

The nerds started to giggle, but I stopped them cold with my dagger stare.

"Hey, Ruby," I said.

We looked at each other for a minute. She twisted a strand of her curly hair around a finger. I coughed into my hand, politely.

"So," I said, "What's up?"

"I saw what you did to those jerky jockstraps," she said. "I never thought . . . well, you didn't seem like . . . I guess I don't know you very well."

"Look, I didn't . . . " I started to explain all over again that it wasn't me, but stopped.

Ruby was wearing a little jean jumper over a nice red sweater. I never noticed before how pretty she was.

"I just gave 'em what they deserved," I said. "They won't mess with me again."

Ruby looked me straight in the eyes. Hers are green.

"It just made me realize maybe I misjudged you. Maybe we all did," Ruby said.

"Yeah! You tell him, girl," said Lynda, the girl with pigtails and braces on her teeth.

I shot them another Shut Up look and they all went back to grazing their lunch trays.

"I thought maybe you and me," said Ruby, "well, maybe you'd like to go over to Burger Hut with me after school."

I heard the nerds whispering and giggling behind my back. I ignored them.

"Sure, that'd be great," I said.

"Some of my friends will be there. I'll introduce you. They're pretty nice once you get to know them," she said. "We all know how it is to be the new kid."

"Yeah, well, it's been kind of rough, I gotta admit," I said.

That's me, master of the understatement. I wanted to tell Ruby all the strange and horrible things that had been happening since I arrived at this school. I wanted to spill it all.

But I didn't. You don't want to go spilling your guts to the first kid who says something nice to you.

The rest of the day went by in a haze. I don't remember English class. I don't remember science. All I thought about all day was Ruby. Ruby, Ruby, Ruby.

The Burger Hut was about two blocks from the school. You had to cross the baseball field, walk through a clump of trees, and cut through a vacant lot. It was right next to a laundromat.

I was hustling along as fast as my big feet and $150 basketball shoes would take me. But like I said before, I'm not too fast.

By the time I made it across the baseball field, I was starting to sweat. So I slowed down because you do not want to show up on a kinda first date all slimy and pitted out.

I was getting ready to cut through the clump of trees when I heard Ruby's voice.

"STOP! Stop it! Please! I'll scream. Help! Somebody help!"

I pushed through the bushes and found Ruby being pinned against a tree by Huff.

"Poor Ruby," Huff said. "You call for help and look who shows up. It's Pukey Lukey," sneered Huff.

"Huff, let her go," I said.

"Not yet, Puke Breath. I'm not done. You can have her when I'm through."

"I said let go of Ruby. NOW!"

Huff shoved Ruby to the ground. He turned to me with his red eyes narrowed into mean slits.

"Okay," he said. "We'll do it your way. I'll take care of you first, and save the sweetie for last. I need me a new pair of shoes anyway."

I dropped my book bag to the ground.

Huff stepped toward me. His fists were clenched. They looked like two big chunks of rock on the end of his sleeves.

His face was blank. His eyes were empty. A dribble of snot leaked from one nostril.

I took a step backwards. My hands were slippery with sweat. My T-shirt was soaked.

"Okay, Puke. Say your prayers," Huff growled.

The flush of heat swept through me. I felt the familiar hardness in my chest, the rolling and rumbling in my stomach.

"Bring it to me, tough stuff," I snarled in a deep and foreign voice.

Huff lunged at me.

I reached down, grabbed the straps of my book bag, and swung it with all my might.

My book bag, fully loaded, weighs about 10 pounds.

It caught Huff square on the jaw. I could hear the bones in his face break.

He let out an agonizing howl. His hands flew to his face.

When he pulled his hands away, half his face looked as if it had caved in. But his forehead was huge and swollen. He didn't look anything like Huff.

His face was that of a movie monster. Ugly and hideous.

He came at me with fists swinging.

"I'LL KILL YOU!" he bellowed.

I was backpedaling, trying to keep a safe distance between Huff and myself.

I tripped over something and fell backwards. Huff charged toward me, raising his thick black boot to kick me in the ribs.

He must have kicked a rock, because his boot never made it to my ribs. He screamed and collapsed on the ground. His boot looked smashed and stubby.

His face was screwed up in pain. He pulled off his boot and ripped off his sock.

His foot was grossly deformed. It was blunt and toeless.

With a roar, Huff struggled to his feet. I looked up at him and the look on his mangled face horrified me. Hate is stronger than pain.

I could see he meant to stomp me with his

good foot. I rolled away just as his big boot came down where my chest had been a second earlier.

Again, he screamed. His back arched as if he had been clubbed from behind. He fell flat on his face, inches from where I was lying.

"Awwwgggggg!" he cried, clutching his hands together.

Maybe he landed on a broken bottle. Or a rusty piece of metal. I don't know.

But when Huff lifted up his hands, they were crumpled and bloody. His fingers were bent and gnarled. They looked like they'd been crushed by some kind of machine, like the kind that turns old cars into little square cubes of metal.

Terrified, I scrambled to my feet. Huff was still on the ground. He was on his knees, bent over with his head on the ground. His deformed hands were drawn to his stomach.

He cried out again. It was a sound of pure pain and agony. The back of his shirt stretched and bulged. Suddenly there was the sound of splitting cloth.

A hard mound of flesh broke through the shoulders of Huff's shirt.

I glanced at Ruby. Her hands covered her mouth. Her eyes were wide with fear.

This couldn't be happening. It couldn't be real.

But it was.

Huff lay sprawled on the ground, moaning and sobbing amid the trash, weeds and dirt.

I looked around — at Ruby, at Huff. My eyes surveyed the trees and bushes until I saw what I was looking for.

The grin. There it was. That monstrous, hideous grin.

What surprised me was whose face it was on.

Chapter Seventeen

He had been standing behind a tree the whole time. He saw it all.

Mr. Peterson!

He saw me looking at him. He showed me the grin again, then turned and ran away.

That was last week.

Nobody picks on me any more.

When I walk the halls, kids get out of my way.

I am feared. And it feels great.

The day after the fight with Huff, I strolled into Miss Swimmer's class late.

"Well, Mr. Lytle, I see you decided to join us," said Miss Swimmer.

I took my time finding my seat. As I walked up the aisle, guys raised their hands so we could slap palms.

I slid into my seat, and dropped my backpack

to the floor with a loud thump.

I glanced over at Ruby. She smiled at me, then looked away.

"Maybe you'd like to share with us your reason for tardiness," Miss Swimmer said.

She was standing in front of her desk with her hands on her hips. She is a pretty woman.

"Nope. I don't think I would," I said.

The rest of the class cracked up. A couple of my mates exchanged high fives. They know who's in charge here.

Miss Swimmer's eyebrows arched. I could see the annoyance in her face.

"Oh, really now," she said. "Maybe you'd like to march yourself down to Mr. Peterson's office."

"Nope," I said, "I don't think I would. Thanks for asking anyway."

The class snickered. Miss Swimmer simmered. Her face flushed red from her forehead to her neck.

A little vein on the side of her head throbbed. You could see it was about to burst.

"All right, young man. That's enough. Everyone, open your book to chapter three."

Everybody flipped their books open. I didn't bother.

Right away, Miss Swimmer was on my case.

"Lucas, I said open your book to chapter three," she said sternly.

"No thanks," I said. I unfolded a paper clip and started cleaning my fingernails.

Miss Swimmer slammed her book on the desk. It sounded like a rifle shot.

"Okay, mister," she said, "you're coming with me."

She marched up the aisle. I didn't move a muscle. She grabbed my arm to yank me out of my desk.

"Ouch!" she yelled, pulling her hand away from my arm.

She looked at her hand as if she had been burned.

The flesh on her fingertips was bubbling and popping.

Shocked by what she saw, Miss Swimmer gasped and her hands flew to her mouth.

She screamed again. Louder this time. It was the shriek of intense pain.

When she dropped her hands, the skin on her face was scorched with the outline of her fingers. The red marks on her lips bubbled and the flesh seemed to melt.

I watched with the same revulsion and fascination as the rest of the class. Her beautiful face was destroyed. It looked ugly and disfigured.

Miss Swimmer shrieked another blood curdling cry and rushed for the door.

After she was out the door and down the hall, kids started whispering and mumbling to each other.

I grabbed my book bag from the floor and stood up from my desk.

"Class dismissed," I announced.

Everybody cheered. Guys slapped me on the back.

I turned to Ruby and offered my arm.

"May I escort you to your next class, Miss Rogers?" I said.

"Why, I'd be delighted, Mr. Lytle," she said.

On her face was that ghastly grin I have come to love.

Chapter Eighteen

At the school bus stop, the doors folded open. I flicked the butt of my cigarette on the ground. I glanced casually at Billy and then at the ground.

He knew what to do.

With the cast on his broken arm, he pounded the last flicker of life from the cigarette butt.

I climbed the steps of the school bus. Billy was right behind, carrying my book bag.

The school bus driver looked the other way when I got on. The younger kids on the bus shrank away from the aisle as I walked by. A couple of them whimpered like they might start crying.

I leaned over to one, who cowered against the window of the bus. I smiled my nicest smile. He gave me a nervous smile in return.

"BOOO!" I shouted into his face.

The kid shrieked. I think he wet his pants.

Everybody laughed, but nobody laughed as loud as me.

I strolled casually to my seat at the back of the bus. Nobody sits there except for me.

I caught one of the older kids giving me the eye. He used to be one of Billy's buddies. Now he's a loner. He's got no friends at all.

"What's your problem, punk?" I said to the kid.

"Yeah, punk," said Billy, standing behind me, "What's your problem?"

"Nothing," the kid said. "I wasn't doing nothing."

But I did not like the tone in his voice.

"Is that right?" I asked, sarcastically. "Maybe I ought to give you a little of the whammy, a little taste of the New Kid Curse. How would you like that?"

I could see fear creep into his eyes like a furry little animal.

"No thanks," he said. "I'll pass."

"Oh, a smart aleck," I said. "We'll see how smart you feel when your face turns to stone and your bones get soggy and your muscles feel like squirming snakes beneath your skin. Consider yourself cursed."

The bus was engulfed in total silence. I couldn't even hear anyone breathing. The kid I cursed looked as pale as death.

"Ha ha ha! HA!" I laughed.

I found my seat at the back of the bus, sat down, and stretched out my legs.

"Okay," I yelled to the bus driver. "Let's get this heap on the road. We don't want the children to be late for school."

The door closed, the brakes hissed, and the school bus lurched.

Boy, I loved being the New Kid. Luke the Lucky. The Duke of Luke. Mighty Lytle, the King of Curses.

When we reached the school, nobody got up. Nobody left their seats. They waited until I dropped my feet to the floor and slowly made my way down the aisle.

I gave the bus driver a pat on the back.

"Nice job," I said before descending the steps. "Take the rest of the day off. But be back here by three."

The hallway was crowded with noisy kids slamming locker doors and talking. But as I strutted through the hall, a hush fell on everyone I passed.

A group of guys, my boys, fell in behind me. It looked like I was towing a fleet of kids behind me as I made my way down the hallway.

I have a new locker. It's a very nice locker. No scratches, no dents, no rust. It used to belong to Huff.

But it's mine now.

"Lucas. Lucas Lytle."

It was Mr. Peterson.

I looked up at him, then went back to opening my lock.

"I would like a word with you," he said. "Step into my office, please."

I turned to my gang.

"A private audience with the Big P," I said. "I'm honored. You heard the man say please, didn't you? I respect politeness in adults."

"Lytle, now," said Mr. Peterson, turning on his heels and heading toward his office.

"Sorry, boys, you'll have to fend for yourselves for a few minutes. I've been summoned," I said.

"Go easy on him, Luke," said one of my guys.

The rest of them laughed.

The door to the principal's office was open so I walked right in. Plopped down in the same chair I had trembled in just such a short time ago.

Mr. Peterson was sitting behind his desk, shuffling papers. He looked up and stared me straight in the eyes.

"I've been getting a lot of complaints about you, Lytle. Pushing kids around. Threatening teachers. Intimidating staff personnel," he said.

I looked surprised.

"Moi?" I said, pointing to my chest. "Why, Mr. P, I am shocked and dismayed by these allegations." I tried to hide my smile. "Really, I am."

"I'm not fooling around here, Lytle. I don't like you. I have never liked you. I am suspending you from school for two weeks. Your parents will be notified." He smiled at me. "Good day."

My smile flipped upside down. He can't do this!

I felt the familiar heat rise in my head. My guts contracted. The rage was back.

"You wouldn't," I said coldly.

"Yes I would and yes I am. Now get out of here."

"You will be sorry," I said. "Just like all the rest. You will regret this day. Your pain will never end. I promise you that."

Mr. Peterson stood up and leaned over his desk toward me. He is a pretty imposing man when you are sitting down and he is standing up.

"Listen, Lytle, I don't understand what has been going on here. Some very strange and unfortunate accidents have plagued this school since the first day you showed up here," he said in a deep, disturbing voice. "But you don't scare me. You don't know who you're dealing with here."

I stood up. We were face to face, nose to nose.

"And neither do you."

Chapter Nineteen

Nobody knows exactly what happened.

Some say he slipped.

Some say he jumped.

Some say he was pushed.

I was sitting on the front steps of the school, smoking a cigarette and waiting for my parents to pick me up.

I knew they were going to be mad that I had been suspended from school. They would be even angrier if they saw me smoking a cigarette.

But so what? I had been a goody-goody, and what did it get me?

A big red bull's-eye on my butt, that's what. I was through being an easy target for every punk and tough guy in the school.

Now I was the one everybody had to watch out for.

I was sitting there, practicing blowing smoke out of my nose, when my mom drove up to the school. I flicked the cigarette into the grass.

I was standing up when I heard the scream.

It came from directly overhead. The sound made me jump. It sent a chill through my body like my blood had suddenly turned to ice.

I looked up and saw Mr. Peterson falling from his office window.

He landed with a sickening thud on the grass next to the school steps, just a few feet from where I was standing.

My mother shrieked.

I looked down at Mr. Peterson's broken body on the ground. His legs were twisted in strange angles from his body. Both hands were covering his face.

The car door slammed.

"Oh, my God, what happened!" Mom yelled. "Is he dead? Somebody call an ambulance!"

She ran up to where Mr. Peterson was motionless on the ground. Mom used to be a nurse. Now she types stuff into computers. She carefully rolled Mr. Peterson onto his back.

She was going to give him mouth-to-mouth, but the look on his face made her gasp and pull back.

It was so horrible I had to look away.

Something more than falling two stories to the ground had happened to Mr. Peterson.

His face...it didn't even look like him. It was a face frozen in fright. Whatever he saw before he landed on the ground had scared him so badly that it distorted his features forever.

It was a face of someone who would rather fall from a window than confront whatever it was he saw. Or it was the face of someone who had been forced to leap by something bigger, more powerful, more frightening than Mr. Peterson himself.

I looked up at the second-story window of Mr. Peterson's office.

Standing in the window, looking down at me, was Miss Smathers.

Her face, that kindly secretary's face, was twisted into a maniac's grin.

I looked away when I heard the ambulance's siren. When I looked back up, she was gone.

They loaded Mr. Peterson into the ambulance

and raced away with sirens screaming.

Mom and I drove home in silence.

I couldn't shake the image of Mr. Peterson's terrified face from my head. Or the disturbing image of Miss Smathers standing at the window.

"Luke," Mom said in a small, whispery voice, "what is going on?"

I shook my head and stared out the car door window.

I kept my mouth shut. Inside my head I heard myself say, "I don't know what it is, but it's out of control."

Chapter Twenty

Getting suspended is not so bad. My advice is: try it, you might like it.

I sure did.

Every day, my mom and dad went to work, and I stayed home.

I played Nintendo, watched the Cartoon Channel, smoked cigarettes on the deck.

I had to endure a torturous lecture from my folks about how disappointed they were in me and how I had let the family down and how I had better shape up fast, mister, or I'll be plenty sorry later.

Blah blah blah and blab blab blab.

I shook my head in agreement and looked real sad and sorry.

"We expect a lot more from you, Luke," my father said.

"I know, Dad," I said, "I'm sorry."

"You almost broke your mother's heart," he said.

"I know, Dad. I'm sorry."

"Oh, Lucas, how could you have done such a thing?" my mom said. "What would Gramma and Grandad think if we told them you've been suspended from school?"

"I know, Mom," I said. "I'm sorry."

"This just doesn't seem like something you would do, Lucas. Are you on drugs?"

"No, Mom," I said. "I'm not doing drugs. I just messed up, that's all. It won't happen again."

"It better not, young man," my dad said. "From now on, you just better straighten up and fly right. You understand?"

"Yes, sir," I said.

That went on for a while until they pooped themselves out. Words can wear a person down. Getting a lecture is like getting beaten up with words.

After my parents went to bed, I stayed up and watched David Letterman.

Billy called the next day. He said Mr. Peterson is still in critical condition. They think his body will recover, but his mind's gone. He never closes his eyes, even when he's sleeping.

Ruby called too. We talked for the longest time. I have never met a girl I could talk to about so many things. We like all the same stuff. Same movies, same music. Same TV shows.

I asked her if she wanted to go to see Exterminator Four with me.

"Well, sure," Ruby said, "but aren't you like grounded or anything."

"Aw, don't worry about that," I said. "I can work that out. Just meet me at the Cineplex Friday night."

My first date with a girl. I was so excited all day. I changed my clothes five times, trying to come up with the right look.

I finally decided that all black looked pretty cool.

"You sure you're not on drugs?" Mom said. "You're acting pretty strange, Lucas."

"Chill, Mom," I said. "I'm OK. It's being cooped up inside this house all week. It's making me antsy."

"Well, you better chill yourself," she said. "You're not going anywhere for another week. You do the crime, you do the time."

Yeah, sure. That's what she thinks.

Every Friday, my parents rent a couple of videos, close the door to their bedroom, and you don't see them again until breakfast the next day. It's like a ritual with them.

The minute their door closed, I was out my bedroom window.

My bike was in the bushes behind the garage where I had stashed it.

The night was cool. The air was sweet with the smell of flowers as I rode through the streets to the movie theater.

Ruby was waiting when I got there.

"Hi," she said.

"Hi," I said back.

We held hands.

I don't remember much about the movie. Same old stuff as Exterminator One, Two, and Three. Bodies blown to bits. Lots of high-speed chases. Hardly any talking. Lots of great special effects.

But I remember the smell of Ruby's hair. I remember how soft her fingers felt holding my hand. I remember how my heart was beating so hard just from sitting next to her in the theater for two hours.

Even the popcorn tasted better because I was sharing it with Ruby.

"I had a great time," she said afterwards.

"Me too," I said.

"I miss you at school," she said.

"I'll be back soon," I said.

"I'm glad," she said.

"Me too," I said.

We didn't kiss or anything.

But I knew I was in love. I was still the New Kid at school, but when I was with Ruby I felt like we had known each other since kindergarten.

I would not let anything, or anyone, get between Ruby and me.

I rode home in a happy haze. It was like my bike was riding on clouds.

The light was off in my parents' bedroom, but I could see the blue flicker of the TV screen through the blinds. Good.

I hid my bike behind the garage, opened my bedroom window, and crawled in.

The minute my foot touched the floor, my bedroom light flicked on.

Mom and Dad were standing by the light switch, their arms folded across their chests.

Uh-oh. Busted.

Chapter Twenty-One

"Where . . . have . . . you . . been?"

I thought about how I should answer that question.

I was already in trouble. Big trouble on top of trouble. I had to choose my words carefully. Then I said the wrong thing.

"None of your business."

I don't know what made me say that. They were not the words I had formed in my head. And it was not my voice that said them.

My mother shrieked like I had stabbed her in the chest with a steak knife.

Dad's face turned blood red. He raised a fist. He wanted to kill me.

But something in my face stopped them. I felt the heat in my head and my stomach tightening. A strength I had never felt before swelled up inside every muscle of my body.

I saw them both recoil and step back away from me.

"I do what I want," said the strange voice inside me. "And you can't stop me."

Mom, her face confused and hurt, stepped behind my father. I saw the blood drain from his face.

"We're still your parents, Luke," he said.

"Don't get in my way, Dad," I said.

"We know what you've been up to, Luke," Dad said. "Ruby Rogers' parents called us. I don't know what's gotten into you, son. But you've changed. And we can't let you go on like this."

A smile spread across my face.

They looked so funny, Mom and Dad, huddled together against my bedroom wall. Silly people.

"You don't own me," I said.

It was like spitting in their face.

The rage returned to Dad's face.

"Oh, you don't think so?" he said. "We'll see about that. You're still a kid. We're still your parents whether you like it or not. Until you get that straight, you will not be seeing any more of Ruby Rogers."

He had punched my button.

"YOU CAN'T DO THAT!" I screamed.

I lunged for Dad, my hands reaching for his throat. But they slipped out of my bedroom door before I could reach them.

I grabbed the doorknob, but they had locked me in. I pounded my fists on the door.

"YOU CAN'T STOP ME! YOU HEAR ME?"

I heard my mother's voice on the other side. She was crying.

"Lucas! Lucas! What has happened to you?"

"I HATE YOU! I HATE YOU!" I yelled at her as I pounded on my bedroom door.

Outside my bedroom, my Dad was nailing my window shut.

I was a prisoner in my own home.

Chapter Twenty-Two

Hate is the most powerful emotion. Hate destroys. Hate is eternal.

Hate outlasts love; hate survives generations.

There are people today who still fight the wars of their ancestors. They fight over differences they don't understand. They kill each other for things that happened hundreds of years ago.

The thing that keeps it going is hate.

I know about hate. I know its power. I know what it can destroy. I know how it can kill.

My parents took me to see a shrink. They were desperate. They didn't know anything else to do.

I rode in the back seat of the car. I stared out the car window. I watched the world rush by. Nobody talked.

It was a long ride. And the longer I was sitting in the back seat, the madder I became.

I shifted my gaze from the window to the back of my parents' heads. My eyes fastened on the bald spot poking through my dad's hair.

My fingers coiled into fists. I felt the blood rising from my chest, up my neck and into my head. My stomach started to growl like some angry animal trapped inside me.

I looked at my mother. She was wearing a straw hat with dried flowers on it. She looks pretty in that hat.

Suddenly, I hated that hat.

I was not going to let them do this to me. I was not going to sit back and let them take away this strength, this power, growing inside me.

I could not return to being the meek, helpless little kid. The butt of every joke. The easy target. Everybody's victim. Luckless Luke. The Cursed New Kid.

The truck that hit our car came from nowhere.

It slammed into the passenger side, where Mom was sitting.

It felt like a carnival ride. We were spinning around, the world a blur of color. I heard the screams. I felt the metal of the car bend and buckle. I heard the glass crack and then shatter.

I heard myself laughing hysterically.

I felt nothing. No pain. No panic. No fear.

I was thrown from the car. I felt myself tumbling through the air like I was doing somersaults from the high dive.

I landed on a soft bed of shrubbery. I was dizzy, but unscathed.

Lucky Luke, that's me.

But my parents were pinned inside the car. A crowd of people were rushing to the wreckage. The smell of gasoline was in the air.

Mom! Dad!

I looked at the car, crumpled and twisted, and I knew they must be dead.

I started to stand up, but my legs collapsed. There were people trying to pull open the crushed doors of the car and get to my parents before the gasoline exploded.

The sound of sirens grew louder.

I dragged myself along the ground toward the wreckage.

"Mommy!" I cried. "Dad!"

My legs were lifeless, but I felt no pain. Clawing at the ground with my hands, I pulled myself to the car.

There were too many people crowding around the car. Some were trying desperately to get to my parents. Others were just standing around.

I could not see anything inside the car. Tears blurred my eyes and burned my face as they ran down my cheeks. My body shook with my sobs.

But as I crawled toward the car, the sirens screaming in my ears, my eyes saw the driver's side mirror of the car lying on the asphalt.

Through my tears, I looked at my reflection in the mirror.

The face that looked back was stretched into the horrible grin.

I knew then it had been me all along. I was the curse. I was hatred. I was the devil.

I split the air with a lung scorching scream.

Chapter Twenty-Three

"Lucas, honey, what is it, what's wrong?"

I opened my eyes.

Mom was leaning over my bed, shaking me awake.

I blinked my eyes, still heavy with sleep.

"Mom?"

She stroked my head and brushed the hair from my sweaty forehead.

"My poor baby," she said, smiling down on me. "Are you okay? You had a bad dream."

A dream? Was it all a dream?

I sat up and looked around my room. The first light of morning was coming through the window. Birds were chirping outside.

Mom gave me a hug.

"It's okay, Lucas. I know the move has been hard on you. It's hard on all of us. But this is the last time you'll have to go through this. Dad and I have decided this is where we're going to stay," she said.

She pulled away from our hug and looked me in the eyes. She saw the confusion and fear in my eyes.

"Don't be so scared, Lucas," she said. "Everything will be okay. Everybody gets the jitters the first day. I know it's not easy being the new kid at school. But you'll adjust. You always do."

She patted me on the back.

"Now," she said, "time to get up. Let's get dressed. I've got a nice breakfast waiting for you."

I pulled on a pair of jeans and a shirt feeling like I was still half asleep.

The dream was still inside my head. It seemed too real. I have never had a dream like that in my life.

I washed my face and stared at myself in the mirror. The face I saw was the same one I have lived with all my life. Ears too big. Nose like a ski jump. Blue eyes, one higher than the other.

I smiled at the mirror, and the mirror smiled back. No hideous grin.

A dream. It was just a dream.

"Another day, another school," I said to myself.

Dad was sitting at the breakfast table when I walked in. Mom had a plate of eggs and toast waiting for me on the table.

Dad lowered the paper.

"Hey, sport, ready for school?" he said. "Mom said you had a little nightmare last night."

I laughed. "Yeah, a little one," I said.

"New kid nerves," Dad said. "I feel the same way my first day of work. But we always get over it, don't we?"

"Sure Dad," I said.

I was starving. I wolfed down the eggs, and asked Mom for more toast.

"You don't need to take the bus this morning, if you don't want to, Lucas," Mom said. "I'll drive you the first day."

Oh, great. Bad enough being the new kid. Even worse if your mom's holding your hand the first day.

"No thanks. I like the bus," I said.

"That's my boy," said Dad, sticking his nose back into the paper.

I brushed my teeth. Packed my book bag. I opened my closet, grabbed my new pair of $150 basketball shoes. I was sitting on the bed, tying the laces, when I changed my mind.

I pulled off the basketball shoes and slipped on my old pair.

I want to start off on the right foot at the new school.

"Bye Mom, bye Dad," I said, heading out the door.

"Wait Lucas," Mom said. "Gimme a kiss."

"Oh, Mom," I said, and pecked her on the cheek with my lips.

"Good luck, slugger," Dad said from the kitchen.

It was a beautiful morning. Kids were walking down the street toward the bus stop in pairs and groups. Nobody talked to me, but they all looked OK. A couple of kids even smiled at me.

I smiled back. It seemed like I was going to like it here.

The smile slid off my face when I reached the bus stop. A group of older kids was standing by a tree, smoking cigarettes.

I recognized Billy Butkis right away.

Worst of all, he seemed to know me.

"Well, well, well," said Billy with a sneer. "Look who's here. It's the new kid."